JUV/E
FIC

Modesitt, Jeanne.
The night call.

$12.95

DATE			

© THE BAKER & TAYLOR CO.

THE NIGHT CALL

By Jeanne Modesitt • Pictures by Robin Spowart

VIKING KESTREL

VIKING KESTREL
Published by the Penguin Group
Viking Penguin, a division of Penguin Books USA Inc.,
40 West 23rd Street, New York, New York 10010, U.S.A.
Penguin Books Ltd, 27 Wrights Lane, London W8 5TZ, England
Penguin Books Australia Ltd, Ringwood, Victoria, Australia
Penguin Books Canada Ltd, 2801 John Street, Markham, Ontario, Canada L3R 1B4
Penguin Books (N.Z.) Ltd, 182–190 Wairau Road, Auckland 10, New Zealand

Penguin Books Ltd, Registered Offices: Harmondsworth, Middlesex, England

First published in 1989 by Viking Penguin, a division of Penguin Books USA Inc.
1   3   5   7   9   10   8   6   4   2
Text copyright © Jeanne Modesitt, 1989
Illustrations copyright © Robin Spowart, 1989
All rights reserved

LIBRARY OF CONGRESS CATALOGING-IN-PUBLICATION DATA
Modesitt, Jeanne.   The night call.
Summary: At night when everyone is asleep, Bear and Rabbit
hear Starman's message on the wind and go to meet their friends in a secret world hidden beneath a hollow tree.
[1. Night—Fiction.   2. Animals—Fiction]   I. Spowart, Robin, ill.   II. Title.
PZ7.M715Ni   1989   [E]   89-9075   ISBN 0-670-82500-X

Printed in Japan.
Set in Cloister.

To each other

One night a bright star fell across the deep, dark sky. Starman, who watches over all the stars, saw it fall and whispered a message to the wind.

The wind carried Starman's words to Rabbit and Mr. Bear.

"Bear," whispered Rabbit, "Starman is calling us."

The animals climbed out of the bedroom window and ran up to the old oak tree in the backyard.

They slowly pushed open a secret door in the tree

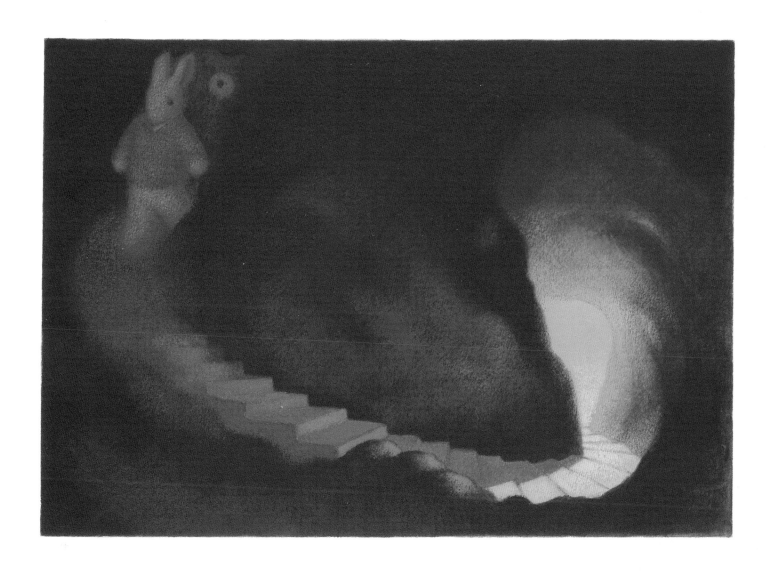

and climbed down the long, winding stairs.

In a few minutes, they came to a large meadow where the sun was shining brightly.

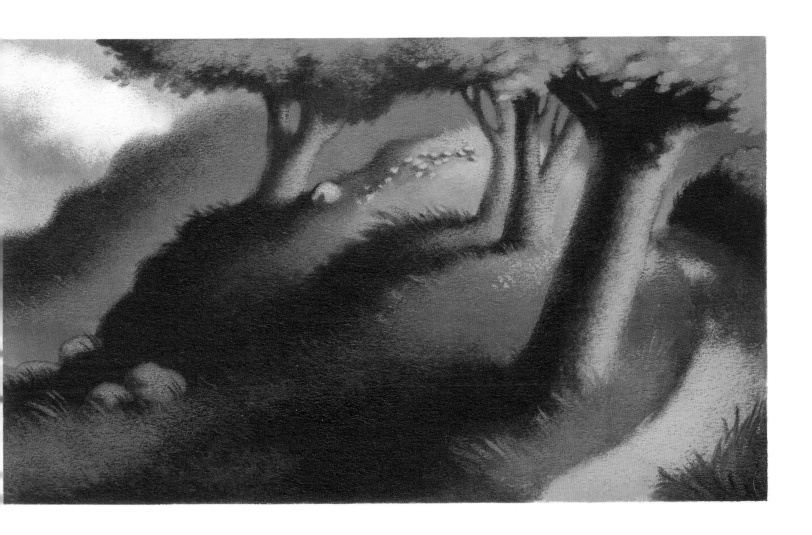

"Hello there!" shouted a voice.

Rabbit and Mr. Bear looked up and saw their friends, Giraffe, Donkey, and Pup. Giraffe handed Rabbit and Mr. Bear each a net.

"We heard Starman's call, too," said Giraffe.

Then they began to search for the fallen star.

They looked along the stream floor and underneath
the water lilies of the pond.

They checked inside the bushes and in the
wavy grasses of the meadow.

Then they climbed all the way up the big mountain.

Finally, they reached the top. Pup spotted something in the distance.

It was a soft light, barely twinkling in the brightness of the sun.
"There it is," Pup shouted. "There's the star."

"Hooray!" cried the happy group and down the mountain they marched and marched

until, at last, the search ended.

There, tangled in the branches of a large, leafy tree, was the fallen star.

Giraffe, being the tallest, gently caught the star in her net.

"Oh, how beautiful," they all said.

Then Rabbit took a deep breath and blew her magic horn.

WHOOSH came the sound of windpaddles. The friends looked up
and saw Starman in his silver-white boat flying toward them.

"Over here!" cried the animals.

Starman guided his boat in the direction of the animals' voices.

"We found it!" shouted the animals.

"Oh, thank goodness," Starman said.

Giraffe lifted the star out of her net and placed it carefully in Starman's hands. Starman, who could only see by night, put the star in his lap and held out his hand to the animals.

"Good job, star-finders," he said. "Now all aboard!" And with Mr. Bear giving directions, away they flew.

Moments later, the boat landed near the stream where the animals had begun their search.

"Good-bye," said the animals as Starman's boat began to sail upwards.
"Farewell, my friends," said Starman. "Until the next star falls."

Rabbit and Mr. Bear said good-bye to Giraffe, Donkey, and Pup, and walked over to the winding stairs, stepped through the tree door, and climbed back into their room.

But before they went to sleep, Rabbit and Mr. Bear looked out of their window. They saw the star they had found. Returned to the night sky by the Starman, it, too, was back home, its light shining more brightly and warmly than ever before.